DISMISSING DEBBIE

Amish Romance

HANNAH MILLER

Tica House
Publishing

Sweet Romance that Delights and Enchants!

Personal Word from the Author

To My Dear Readers,

How exciting that you have chosen one of my books to read. Thank you! I am proud to now be part of the team of writers at Tica House Publishing who work joyfully to bring you stories of hope, faith, courage, and love.

Please feel free to contact me as I love to hear from my readers. I would like to personally invite you to sign up for updates and to become part of our **Exclusive Reader Club** —it's completely Free to join! Hope to see you there!

With love,

Hannah Miller

VISIT HERE to Join our Reader's Club and to Receive Tica House Updates:

https://amish.subscribemenow.com/

Chapter One

Debbie glanced behind her, back at the rolling pasture in the distance, dotted with sheep. The hedgerow that bordered the road was thick with blackberry briars. Jonas laughed. "Come on, Debs, what are you afraid of?" he said.

Debbie glared at him. He was standing in front of the barn, an old, derelict thing that looked as though it could crumble into dust at any moment. His arms were loose at his sides, his dark curls lifting slightly in the late summer breeze. His eyes twinkled with merriment, and that smile—it was his smile that Debbie could never say no to.

"I'm not afraid of anything," she told him, and he laughed again.

"*Gut*," he said, and held out his hand. She took it, enjoying the feel of his warm, calloused skin against hers, and followed him into the barn.

It smelled of old straw and mildew in the barn, of rot and dust. Not exactly romantic. But it was private, hidden away. They could be alone here, talk without anybody listening, without anybody judging.

Jonas settled onto an old haystack that sent up a little cloud of dust as he sat down. Debbie took a spot opposite him and neatened out her skirts around her.

She glanced upwards, at the roof. There were holes in it, sunlight filtering through, highlighting dust motes that danced around them. A couple of the beams looked rotten.

"Are you sure this is safe?" she asked.

Jonas followed her gaze upward, then shrugged. "This barn's been here for years, Debs. It'll be here a few more yet."

He had a point, she thought.

Jonas began to unpack the bag he'd brought with him. He unloaded sandwiches, fruit, and some kind of cookies onto a small cloth, and offered it all to her. She took a sandwich, eating slowly. In the time it took her to eat one, he'd already wolfed down three.

"I'll be right back," he said, dusting crumbs off his pants as he stood. "Just want to check on the horse. I don't like it when he's this quiet."

He was only gone a moment, and then he was back.

"Still there," he said. "Not that Bandit could go very far even if he did get loose. Honestly, *Mamm* should sell him off. Wouldn't get very much, but he eats far too much for the little work he actually does."

"Poor Bandit," Debbie said, although she was smiling. "He has to carry you around all day, I shouldn't wonder he's tired."

Jonas rolled his eyes. "You want him, Debs? Hmm? Going for $300. No takers? All right, 250. Can I get 200? Anyone for 200?" He jumped on the bale of hay. It wobbled precariously under his feet. "Come on, excellent breed. Old and lazy but a good color standard, still intact. Can I get 150?"

Debbie was laughing now, holding her sides to stop herself doubling over. "Jonas, stop!" she protested.

Instead, he jumped higher onto the stacked bales, then hauled himself up into the loft. He stood there, legs parted, hands on his hips. "On hundred dollars for the old sod," he declared. "Any takers?"

Something creaked, then cracked. Debbie shrieked. "Jonas Peachey, get down from there! The whole thing's going to give way!"

"Relax," he said, but he was already climbing down from the loft. "You worry too much, Debs."

She was about to argue when a sharp *crack* cut through any

reply she might have had. She screamed as a beam came loose, falling down into the barn, separating her from Jonas. Loud creaking told her the rest of the barn was coming down, too.

"Jonas!" she screamed, but she couldn't hear him, couldn't see him. She darted for the exit.

Dust clouded around her as the roof caved in.

Jonas ran, the barn crumbling behind him. His heart hammered in his chest. Bandit had bolted, dragging the buggy with him. Jonas paused, but only for a moment ... he had to catch that horse. And Debbie had hollered at him, so she was all right. If the horse raced into traffic and got killed... Why, Jonas would be killed, too—by his dad. He took off running, chasing after the cursed horse, shouting and waving his arms. The horse would race into traffic—he was just stupid enough...

Eventually, Jonas caught up to him. Bandit was munching on a patch of long grass, as though nothing had happened at all.

Jonas frowned and jumped up into the buggy, driving it back toward town. He couldn't see any sign of Debbie. She must have decided to walk back—her family's farm wasn't far in the other direction. What a way for their afternoon to turn out—he'd had such high hopes. Debbie was likely to be vexed with him now. He'd catch it from her when he saw her again.

He smiled. He did like the girl. She had spirit, and she laughed at all his jokes. He'd make arrangements to see her again right soon. In the meantime, he'd catch it if he didn't get the horse and buggy back real quick-like. And he wasn't in the mood to hear one of his father's unending lectures.

For a moment, he thought maybe he should mention the barn to someone. But no—no one needed to know he and Debbie had been there. What if they were blamed for the collapse? But that thing was a relic, ancient. It had been bound to fall down at some point or other.

Likely, Debbie wouldn't tell anyone they'd been there, either. He probably should have listened to her in the first place. That barn was a menace. *Ach*, but she was going to be put out with him, for sure and for certain.

He wondered if he should turn back and try to intercept her before she got home. Nah, she was almost certain to be home by then, and he didn't think it would be seemly to ride up to her porch and ask to see her. He chuckled. He'd better give her time to cool off before he went around again. Maybe tomorrow. She'd surely be over it by morning. She never was one to hold grudges.

Debbie's twin sister Dawn was sweeping the kitchen when Noah Eicher rushed in, door banging off the wall behind him. He was out of breath, his blond hair slicked back. She stared at him, wondering what on earth could have happened for him to run into their house like this.

"Sorry," he said, taking a step back from her. "Sorry—but Dawn, is anyone else here? I've got the Rabers out, but there's only Ellen there and oh—" He was tripping over his words, not making much sense.

Dawn was quickly losing patience with the gangly sixteen-year-old. "Spit it out, Noah," she said, both exasperated and worried.

"That old barn, you know the one, on Josiah Hilty's farm, it's just fallen down, and I thought—I thought I heard someone shouting from inside. We need all the help we can get. I'm trying to tell everyone..."

Dawn set down her broom and quickly hurried into the sitting room where her mother was mending clothes.

"Noah says the old barn on the Hilty farm's come down." She frowned. Noah was well known for his tendency to exaggerate, so she didn't know how much of an emergency this really was. More than likely, there was no one in there at all. But still ... if there was even a chance someone was trapped. "He thinks there's someone in there."

Susanna Shelter set aside her mending and got right up. "I'll fetch your father. You go quickly with Noah and see what you can do."

Dawn nodded and followed Noah a good piece down the road

to the old barn. There were already a few people gathered there. They were moving pieces of wood, trying to clear it away.

"What's going on?" she asked Isaac Farmer, who was stood a little back from the crowd, no doubt too young to be of much help.

"There's someone trapped inside," he said, lisping the words.

Dawn gasped. Noah hadn't been exaggerating after all. "Who? Who is it?"

Isaac shook his head. "I don't know. A girl, I think."

Dawn hurried forward to help clear away the rubble, moving smaller pieces of wood and helping the men with the larger pieces. Even then, in the back of her mind, she couldn't help wondering, *Where's Debbie?*

She hadn't seen her twin sister since breakfast that morning, which was unusual. And Debbie *had* said she was going out for a walk. Surely, she wouldn't have walked out here, though, and gone into this horrible old barn all by herself?

No, Dawn assured herself. Debbie was fine. In fact, she'd probably show up with *Mamm* and *Dat* any second now.

And then she saw it, a swatch of reddish-brown hair, a pale, curled hand. Someone moved aside the beam of wood lying across her, and the figure shifted. *Debbie.*

Dawn screamed and flung herself over her sister, feeling for a pulse, anything.

Debbie groaned, and Dawn pulled back, gasping with relief. She quickly looked her sister up and down. Debbie was dusty and bruised, but one leg was still underneath a second beam. There was blood, and was that a *bone* poking through the skin?

"Help!" Dawn cried. "Help her!"

The men rushed around and tried to lift the beam from Debbie's leg.

Dawn felt as though she was going to throw up. She could hear sirens in the distance—thank *Gott* someone had thought to run to the phone shanty out on the main road and call the emergency services.

"Debbie?" Dawn said, her voice shaking, tears hot in her eyes. "It's going to be okay, Debbie. I promise," she said, stroking her sister's hair, the same reddish-brown as her own.

Gott, she prayed. *Please, please, please let my sister be okay.*

Chapter Two

Dawn couldn't meet her parents' eyes. All of them were looking anywhere but at each other, each lost in their own fears. Dawn's knee was bouncing up and down and her hands were fisted in her apron. Debbie was still in surgery. What were they doing to her in there? Dawn needed to know, needed to know that Debbie was going to be okay. She couldn't die—she just *couldn't*. On the stretcher Dawn had heard Debbie murmur something. That meant, surely, she would be okay. She was conscious and talking.

And she would feel it, wouldn't she? If Debbie died in surgery, Dawn would feel it. She'd heard of that happening with twins. And she hadn't felt anything like that, so... Debbie had to be okay. Why hadn't anyone come to tell them that yet?

Time seemed to drag, almost like being frozen. Nothing

existed outside this hospital. There was only this room, and Debbie, off in some unknown surgical room, with bright lights and doctors with scalpels. Dawn shuddered at the thought. And then, the door opened. All three of them stood, and the doctor came forward.

He cleared his throat, brushing a wisp of blonde hair back from his face. "I just came to let you know, Deborah's come through surgery. The surgery went well, but..." he faltered then, and Dawn's heart froze. "We had to amputate part of her left leg. The damage was extensive, and it couldn't be saved. But we're confident she'll make a full recovery and..."

He trailed off at the sight of *Dat's* face, fury that was quickly covered over the moment the doctor stopped speaking. There were tears in *Mamm's* eyes. Dawn was grateful her sister was alive. As far as she was concerned, they could worry about anything else later.

"When can we see her?" she asked.

The doctor inhaled deeply. "As soon as you like," he said. "She's still sleeping off the anesthetic, but you can sit with her."

The doctor led them down pristine, chemical-scented corridors and through a set of double doors with sanitizer dispensers on either side of them. Dawn washed her hands and followed her parents through into the room. There were four beds in the room, two unoccupied, one with curtains drawn all the way around it, and there, in the last bed, beside the window, was Debbie.

Her face was turned away from them, her hair spread loose around her shoulders and over the white pillow.

Mamm was the first to her side. Dawn fought the tears burning her eyes. Now she'd seen her, now she knew Debbie was alive, so there was no reason to cry. *Was there?* But the tears forced their way down her cheeks. She was ready to burst into tears. But Debbie needed sleep. And *Mamm* needed to be close to Debbie.

Dawn said a silent prayer and stepped outside into the corridor. She couldn't be in there. Not yet. She needed to get ahold of herself. She sucked in a breath, eyeing the vending machine more for something to do than because she actually wanted anything. Maybe if she walked a bit. Debbie knew her all too well. If she went back into her room, Debbie would know how upset she was and then she'd be worse off. No. Dawn needed to leave her alone for a bit.

She started walking, blinking back her tears and eventually came to a small café. She sat in a corner without buying anything. No one bothered her, and she sat there for a while, staring out of the window before *Dat* found her and sat down opposite her.

She forced a smile when she looked at him, but she didn't feel it. The truth of what her sister would face was becoming all too real. How could Debbie get on with only one leg? This would affect her whole life—it would affect *everything*. Dawn's heart broke for her sister.

Dat's dark eyes were stern, his mouth a thin line. Had those creases in his face been there before? They seemed multiplied, somehow.

"Your sister's awake," he said. "Well, in and out of it really. But you know... the leg..."

Dawn nodded. *The leg.*

"She's going to need a lot of help when she comes home."

"I know that," Dawn said, her voice shaking. Was her dad asking if she would help? Why would he need to ask? Of course, she would help. She would do anything for her sister.

"*Gut*," he said, leaning back in his seat, his shoulders sloping. "*Gut*."

"I'm ready to see her now," Dawn said.

Her father waved his hand, a 'go ahead' sort of gesture, and Dawn eased out of her seat, heading off in the direction she'd come from. Her dad didn't follow her.

Mamm glanced up as Dawn came up beside her. "I'll watch her for a bit," she said. "*Dat's* in the café. You should get a cup of tea or something."

She half-expected *Mamm* to argue, but instead she nodded, stood, and walked off in the direction Dawn indicated. Dawn took her seat, leaning forward and brushing Debbie's hair with her fingers.

Debbie groaned then, a groggy sort of sound. Then she turned her head, and her eyes blinked opened. "Dawn?" she said. She sounded tired, like she'd just woken up from a very long sleep. "Where am I? Wh-where's Jonas?"

Jonas? Why was she asking about Jonas? Did she mean Jonas Peachey? Yes, of course she must, for hadn't they been seeing each other for a few weeks now?

"Do you want me to send for him?"

"Is he okay?" Debbie asked, her eyes filling with tears. "Is he..." she trailed off then, her eyes fluttering closed. Just like that, she was asleep.

Is he okay? That question nagged at Dawn even hours later, after she and *Dat* had gone home, leaving *Mamm* at the hospital with Debbie.

Chapter Three

It was dark outside the windows, but the hospital ward was brightly lit with artificial light. Debbie's eyes opened, and she squinted against the lights until her vision cleared. Ah, yes. She remembered this room, those ugly plastic curtains.

Mamm was asleep in the chair beside the bed, her head tipped back, her mouth open, snoring. Debbie would have laughed if she weren't so scared.

What had happened back at the barn? Was Jonas okay? She didn't know.

She licked her lips, craving water. There was some on the stand beside her bed, and she reached for it. Thirst quenched, she became more aware of the throbbing pain in her left leg, a dull ache just above the knee.

She was about to wake her *mamm* when the curtains drew back with a rattling sound. She expected to see a nurse, doing their rounds, but instead it was Dawn standing there.

"You're awake," she said, her voice low—probably to avoid waking their mother. She moved a little closer to the bed. Her *kapp* was slightly askew and she wore a pained expression, like she was holding something back.

"Where's Jonas?" Debbie asked. She wanted to see him, needed to know he was all right.

Dawn shook her head. "He's not here."

"Is he—" Debbie cleared her throat and tried again. "Was he injured? In the barn?"

"He wasn't in the barn when it collapsed. Some of the men pulled it all apart. And besides, Noah says he saw him in town yesterday."

"But why—"

"I don't know," Dawn said, answering Debbie's question before she'd even finished asking it. She sounded annoyed, almost angry, on Debbie's behalf. Debbie loved her a bit for that.

"How do you feel?" Dawn asked then, shifting the subject away from Jonas.

Debbie wasn't sure how to answer that. She felt strange,

drugged, weighed down. The pain in her leg wasn't getting any better, either.

"I'll go and find a nurse, get them to explain things to you," Dawn said, and then she vanished behind the curtain.

Debbie wanted to call out, to beg her to come back. She didn't want to be in this room alone. But she wasn't alone. *Mamm* was beside her, albeit asleep.

Explain what, exactly? she thought. She'd only been in the hospital once before in her life, when she was young. She could barely remember it. She had no idea how things were done, what kind of things might need explaining. Was something wrong with her? She didn't feel wrong. Except, that throbbing pain was only getting worse. And it *looked* wrong, like... like there was nothing there, under the sheet.

Grimacing, she threw back the covers to see what was going on.

She screamed, then, a loud, wailing sound that rose up from somewhere deep inside her. She couldn't breathe, couldn't think, her brain was shutting down and pure fear taking over her body.

Mamm's voice, then, soothing, like it always had been. Debbie stopped screaming, but she still couldn't quite get hold of her thoughts. She did as her mother told her, breathing in and out, deep breaths, but it didn't change anything. Half her left leg was missing, her thigh ending above the knee with nothing below, wrapped in bandages.

She thought she might vomit.

The doctor came then, explaining things in terms she barely understood. She couldn't listen, couldn't even really hear what he was saying, but *Mamm* and Debbie both nodded, asking questions. They were listening for her.

Debbie lay back against the pillows, closed her eyes, and pretended she was somewhere else. None of this was real. She was still at home, feeding the chickens, watering the vegetable garden. Jonas was waiting for her at the end of the drive, a bunch of posies in his hand.

Jonas. Where was he? Why wasn't he here, at her bedside? From Dawn's reaction, Debbie was sure he hadn't been to the hospital at all, hadn't even asked to see her. *Why?* she thought. And he was seen in town afterward? Dawn had assured her he was fine, that he hadn't been in the barn, but... It sounded like he hadn't even been there when she'd been found. What had happened to him?

Dawn slept by Debbie's bedside that night. She woke with a stiff back, her clothes crumpled and her *kapp* askew. She sorted herself out, hurrying to the bathroom to wash her face and brush her teeth with a toothbrush she'd found on the hospital nightstand. She looked rough, but then, she *felt* rough. Although not half as bad as Debbie must feel, she reminded herself quickly.

Debbie had told her everything last night, that she'd been at the barn with Jonas, that she was worried about him. Dawn had asked their parents, quietly, to see if they could find him, but they'd so far come up empty.

Debbie murmured something and turned her head away from Dawn, still half-asleep. She was on heavy painkillers, and she was sleeping most of the day. That was good, the nurse had said. More sleep meant more time healing.

"What time is it?" Debbie asked, then, her words slurred with sleep.

There was no clock at this end of the ward, so Dawn had to walk to the far end near the exit to check. It was a little past eight in the morning.

She could see *Dat* through the small square windows in the doors, talking to someone. She stepped back as he pushed the doors open, followed by the Peacheys—Jonas included.

Dawn stared at him, but he didn't meet her gaze. He hung back a bit from his family, walking just slightly behind his older brother, Jacob. It wasn't like Jonas to be quiet, but it seemed as though all the confidence had been knocked out of him.

Maybe that was because of Debbie though—she was badly

injured. Jonas was probably worried. That didn't explain why he hadn't come to visit over the past couple of days, but still. He was there now. Perhaps that was what mattered.

Debbie was sitting up in bed when Dawn hurried back to duck through the curtains to tell her the Peacheys were here. "And Jonas?" Debbie couldn't help but ask.

Dawn assured her he was here, and helped her to fix her *kapp*. They couldn't do much about anything else, but at least Debbie felt less on show with her hair tied back and covered.

A few minutes later, Mary and Abraham Peachey walked in, followed by Jacob, and then, trailing behind, Jonas. Debbie wanted to cry with delight, to ask where he'd been, to fuss over him and make sure he was all right, but of course she didn't—couldn't, not with other people there.

"*Ach*, Debbie, goodness, look at you," Mary said, coming to sit down beside her. "*Gott* will give you strength, I'm sure."

Her words were nowhere near as comforting as she probably meant them to be. Did she really look that bad? She didn't want to be pitied.

Mary reached for her hand and Debbie let her take it. She'd always gotten the feeling that Mary didn't like her all that much. She was nice enough, always civil, but there was something in her voice, even now, that put Debbie on edge, that made her feel like she was being judged, though for what, Debbie had no idea.

"We'll be praying for you, I promise," Mary told her, and that at least, Debbie was glad of. Right now, she needed all the prayers she could get. Not that it would give her back her leg —no, that was gone. But she *did* need God's help if she was going to get through this.

But she was sure she would. Life was hardship, but it was fleeting, and heaven was everlasting. And besides, she had her family around her, to support her, and Jonas was here.

Jonas. Who wasn't meeting her gaze, who was looking everywhere but at her.

"God has already worked a miracle," Debbie said. "I'm alive, and Jonas is okay."

Mary frowned. "Jonas?" She glanced back at her son, who shrugged, and then again at Debbie for clarification.

"Must be the morphine," Jonas said, in that dismissive tone of his that she'd heard many times. "I'm guessing she's on a lot of it, right?" he asked Dawn.

She? Why was he talking like Debbie was hardly even in the room? Why wasn't he telling the truth? Confused, Debbie let the room fade away, trying to make sense of it. Her mind felt damp, like it was full of wet wood pulp. Maybe she hadn't understood quite right, or she hadn't said quite what she'd meant to. She *was* on a fair bit of morphine, after all.

Mary stood, bringing the visit to an end. How long had they been here? Five minutes? Ten? They'd come all this way, and they were in such a hurry to be going again.

Debbie was tired; she needed to sleep. She didn't say anything, just watched as they left the ward, then buried herself back beneath her bedsheets, and slept.

"Jonas?" Dawn called as the Peacheys filed out of the ward. Mary and Abraham were talking with her parents, so she figured now was a good time. "Can I speak to you for a moment?"

Jonas shrugged. "Sure," he said, and followed her down the corridor. They were in sight of their families, but just out of hearing, Dawn made sure.

"You were in that barn with Debbie when it came down, weren't you?" Dawn said, injecting a little steel into her voice. "Why didn't you say so? Why weren't you there when everyone was trying to dig her out?"

Jonas frowned. "I've no idea what you're talking about," he said. "I was nowhere near that barn. In fact, I think I was running errands in town when it happened. I was late back that day, so I didn't even hear about it until nightfall."

Dawn clenched her jaw. She wanted to shout, to call him a liar outright. Instead, she said, "I could have sworn Debbie said you were there. She was so worried about you, too."

"*Nee*," Jonas said firmly, almost rudely. "I was never there. Debbie must have got it wrong. Like you said, she's on a lot of morphine."

"*I* never said that," Dawn reminded him. "You did. And she was very clear. But of course, if you say you weren't there..."

He was lying. Dawn wanted to slap him, to wipe that vacant look off his face. But no... She wouldn't do that. She wasn't violent. She was the better person here, no matter what he was inadvertently saying about Debbie, implying that she was either confused or lying, no matter that *he'd left her there.*

"She could have died, you know," Dawn said, her tone cutting. "The doctors said she was very lucky. If she'd been found any later, she might have died just from the blood loss."

Jonas' face went white, then, and Dawn was glad to see some sort of expression on his face, even if it wasn't honest or apologetic. He felt bad, then, at least. That was something.

"Then thank *Gott* she's all right," he said.

Dawn nodded. "*Jah, Gott* is always watching over us."

As he turned and walked back down the corridor, Dawn spotted Jacob watching them, his eyes narrowed. Had he heard their conversation? Well, if he had, that was Jonas's problem, not hers. She had bigger things to worry about.

Chapter Four

Debbie was released from the hospital three days later. She got off her family's cart awkwardly and with much leaning on her parents for support. She wasn't very skilled at using her crutches, and Debbie wondered if they weren't more a bother than a help. But she couldn't think of that now. She *wouldn't* think of that now. All the talking from the doctors and the nurses and the specialists in the hospital echoed in her head, circling and circling until it all became a noisy gong. Advice. Therapy. Crutches. Walker. A false leg...

No. She couldn't think of it right then.

She supposed she was going to have to depend on others again, like she was a child. The thought irked her, and she wanted nothing more than to be alone.

Jonas hadn't come back to see her. Debbie wasn't sure why—guilt, maybe? Or perhaps he hadn't had time... But no, if he'd wanted to see her, he would have made the time. In which case, it had to be the leg. She must repulse him now. She could no longer keep up with him, no longer run through the fields with him or help him load hay onto his cart. She'd never be normal to him.

Her *mamm* helped her to her room, and there Debbie stayed for several days, eating meals in her bed, staring out the window when she could summon enough strength to use her crutches to get to the window seat.

Days later, Dawn knocked on her door, letting herself in without waiting for an answer, as was her habit. Back at their house in Wisconsin, they'd shared a room, and now both treated each other's rooms as if they belonged to both of them.

"Oh *gut,* you're up," Dawn said, as if she was surprised.

Debbie had managed to get out of bed by herself that morning, although she hadn't bothered to dress and was still in her nightclothes. She was sitting in the window seat, her good leg outstretched, just how the nurse had told her to keep it.

"I'm up," Debbie confirmed, although really, she wasn't sure what the point of being out of bed was—it wasn't as though she could do anything.

"Are you ready to do your exercises?"

Debbie scowled. She hated it when Dawn talked like she was *Mamm*. It was a new attitude for her. Before, they had always been equals. Now, something had shifted. Dawn wasn't just her sister anymore, her friend. She was her care-giver. But Debbie nodded anyway. She had to do it, she supposed, if she ever wanted to be useful again. More than that, she had to do it if she wanted Dawn and the rest of them to leave her alone.

"Have you heard from Jonas?" Debbie asked, as Dawn knelt and helped her to stretch her leg.

Dawn shook her head. "You're better off without him, Debs. Trust me."

Debbie studied her sister. Dawn knew something. "What aren't you telling me?"

Dawn sighed and sat back on her heels. "He tried to tell me he wasn't at the barn. I know he was lying. And I'm sure he knew I knew it, too, but he won't admit being there."

Debbie's mouth fell open, but no words came out. Eventually, she managed to stutter a small, "Why?"

Dawn shrugged. "Because he's not a good person, Debbie. I

don't know why other than that. I'm sorry. I know you liked him."

Debbie laughed then. *Liked?* It was much more than that. She *loved* Jonas. She would have married him, if he'd asked her. That was her future—a family with Jonas. Wasn't it?

No, she thought. No, it wasn't. Jonas didn't want her to see her now, didn't want to admit to ever being with her at the barn.

Am I really so awful? she wondered. *What's wrong with me?* She glanced down at the stump of her leg and quickly looked away again. *Oh*, she thought. *That.*

She let Dawn help her clean her stump, avoiding looking at it the whole time, and let out a sigh of relief when Dawn finally left her alone.

Alone. That was what she was now. What she wanted, even. To be alone. Who wanted to be around her now, really? Debbie sighed and rested her head back against the wall. Everything had changed. Nothing would ever be the same again.

Jacob hadn't been able to look at his brother for days. Jacob loved his brother, he did, but right now Jonas was nothing but a disappointment. There was no backbone in him. Jacob had always known that, he supposed. How many times had he caught Jonas in a lie? But never a lie like this. Pretending he hadn't been at that barn with Debbie, and all because he didn't want them to know they'd been courting in secret. Trying to save his own skin, as usual. It made Jacob ill.

He pulled the buggy up in the Shelters' driveway, less bumpy now that Joseph and Susanna had redone it, put down new gravel. It must have taken them at least a day to do all that work. They'd done it for Debbie, he supposed, to make getting around easier for her. He noticed a new handrail beside the steps up to the porch, too. At least someone was looking out for Debbie, even if Jonas wasn't.

He knocked on the door, and Dawn answered it. Her face lit up into a smile, and he was glad at that. He'd worried that perhaps he might not be welcome, after how his brother had treated Debbie. But Dawn ushered him in and gestured to a seat at the kitchen table, busying herself with making him tea.

"How's Debbie?" he asked. He didn't know if Debbie wanted to see him or not, but he hadn't been able to stay away. He needed to know how she was, especially after knowing what Jonas had done, leaving her alone like that. She might have *died*, and that, he was sure, would have been on Jonas.

"She's starting to recover," Dawn said, but there was something cautious in her voice. "As much as she can, anyway."

"But...?" he asked, unsure whether he should be pressing the matter or not. He knew that, really, it was none of his business.

"But... Oh, well. I suppose she's just not really herself at the moment. I mean, it's been quite an ordeal."

Quite an ordeal. That was an understatement if ever he'd heard one. "Is she taking visitors?" he asked, thinking that perhaps he might cheer her up somehow.

"I don't know if she will, but I can ask."

Jacob thanked her and waited while she hurried upstairs. He sipped his tea slowly, wondering what on earth he could say to Debbie to 'cheer her up'. Perhaps he shouldn't even try. Jokes probably weren't appropriate at the moment.

When Dawn returned, she only shook her head. "She doesn't want to see anyone. I'm sorry." She sounded genuinely apologetic, too.

He drained the last of his tea and raised a hand. "No apologies needed. I didn't really think she would. I just wanted to know how she was doing." He stood, then had a thought. Maybe, somehow, he could make things a little bit right again. "Look, is there anything I can help with? I don't know, take on some of Debbie's duties, or pick things up from the town for you?"

Dawn seemed to consider it for a moment. "Not right now, but I'll ask *Mamm* and *Dat* and let you know if we need anything. Thank you."

She showed him out the door, closing it behind him. He climbed up onto the buggy and urged old Bandit into motion. If he could help, even just a little bit, that would be something, he supposed. Perhaps he'd come back tomorrow. He wouldn't ask to see Debbie, not if she didn't want to see him; he could just see how she was doing, and whether the Shelters needed anything.

Chapter Five

Dawn helped her down off the cart. Debbie was getting better at balance now, and although she leaned heavily on Dawn, she didn't stumble.

"The doctor sounded very positive," Dawn said, and for once, Debbie agreed. They'd spoken about a prosthesis, hardly the same as having a whole leg again—but it was something, Debbie thought, something to make her feel a little bit normal again. And it would help with her balance, too.

Maybe it would help Jonas feel like things were a bit more normal. She couldn't help feeling as though, if she could just talk to him, discuss things and let him know that it wasn't the end of her usefulness, just a setback, then maybe he would see. Maybe he would realize that it wouldn't be everything on his shoulders, that they could face this new disability together.

Debbie wasn't helpless. She refused to be that, ever. But she *did* need help. The difference was, perhaps, a subtle one, but one she felt she could make Jonas understand. If only she could talk to him. She could tell him that she didn't blame him, that it wasn't his fault. She understood that he'd been scared and hadn't wanted anyone to think it was his fault.

"Dawn," she said, before they went inside. "Do you think you could do something for me?"

Dawn turned her head. Her grip shifted around Debbie's waist, but didn't slacken. "Depends what it is," she said.

"I need to speak with Jonas. Do you think you could arrange that?"

Dawn's expression shifted into a frown. Debbie knew exactly what Dawn thought of Jonas now, but she also knew that her sister wouldn't deny her something like this, not when it was so important to her. "Please, Dawn," she said.

Dawn sighed. "I suppose so."

Debbie leaned her head against Dawn's shoulder. "Thank you," she said, "For this, and for everything else."

Dawn merely let out a slight grunt of acknowledgement. Debbie almost laughed. "I'm glad you're my sister," she said.

"Me, too," Dawn said, and there was nothing but honesty in

those words.

Together, they headed inside.

It was another week before Dawn managed to arrange for Debbie to see Jonas. Debbie asked every day, not meaning to be pushy, but too desperate not to be. That morning she dressed fully, tying back her freshly washed hair and donning her *kapp*. She looked good, she thought, better than she had since... since it had happened. Healthy, even. She'd been eating better the last few days, able now to manage full meals instead of just picking at them, and she'd been crying less, so her face wasn't as puffy, her eyes less shadowed and red-rimmed. She looked almost like herself again.

Gott, please let this work, she prayed silently. *We're meant to be together. I know it.* She made her way out of her room, and Dawn helped her down the stairs. *Dat* was fixing up the sewing room on the main floor, with the help of Jacob Peachey, so that she could move in there when it was done. It was a smaller room, with not so nice a view, but it would make things easier.

"Where are you girls off to?" *Mamm* asked as she spotted them in the hallway.

Debbie glanced at Dawn. Where *were* they going? Dawn hadn't actually told her the location of this meeting.

"I thought it would be good to go for a short stroll before Debbie's appointment in town," Dawn said.

"But she still has trouble with her crutches," *Mamm* protested. "She's not ready for a stroll."

"She needs to get out a bit, *Mamm*. Please," Dawn said. "I'll help her. You know I will."

Debbie could have kissed her. Not that she really approved of lying, but she certainly didn't want her parents knowing she was off for a secret meeting with Jonas Peachey.

"I didn't lie," Dawn said once they were outside. "Well, not entirely. We *are* going for a short walk."

Debbie tried not to be nervous. She hadn't done much walking since the incident, for obvious reasons. She'd used her crutches to get about the house and had stood out on the porch a few times, never more than a yard or two away from the front door.

"Only a short one," Dawn assured her. "You'll manage."

Debbie wasn't so sure, but she had faith in her sister if not completely in herself. Besides, she was desperate to talk to Jonas.

Dawn pulled the cart to a stop by the riverbank and helped Debbie down. It was flat ground there, easy to navigate. The breeze was cool and fresh on Debbie's face, and the sounds of the ducks quacking amongst the reeds was soothing.

And there, sitting on a bench near the water, was Jonas.

Debbie's heart leapt. She wanted to run to him, to leap into his arms. *Good luck trying,* she thought bitterly, then scolded herself. She shouldn't think like that, shouldn't be so hard on herself. Things were hard enough without her internal critic getting involved, too.

Debbie set off toward him on her crutches, Dawn walking beside her. Debbie was glad for her sister's company. She wasn't sure she'd hold it together without her. Now, or at all, over the past couple of weeks.

She reached the bench, but although Jonas glanced up at her and nodded, he didn't speak. She settled herself down on the bench, wondering why he was so quiet. It wasn't like Jonas to be quiet.

"I'll be just over there," Dawn said, gesturing back to where she'd parked the pony cart. It was a short way off, in sight but well out of hearing distance for a normal conversation. "Shout if you need me."

Debbie nodded. As Dawn walked away, Debbie couldn't help but feel a little nervous.

"Jonas," she began, but stopped. His expression was shuttered. There was nothing there of the Jonas she knew, the Jonas she loved. No amusement, no fondness, just blankness.

"How are you?" he asked, but it sounded insincere, like he didn't really care one way or the other about the answer.

Why did he seem so cold? He was usually the opposite, warm, always smiling and full of jokes. But now...

Debbie breathed in, summoning the strength not to crumble under Jonas' cold gaze.

"Better," she said. "I'm almost used to it now." Now *that* was a lie. "I'm relearning a lot of things, but I'm getting there. I plan to be helping out with the chores again by the autumn."

Jonas nodded. "*Gut*. That's *gut*."

"Look," Debbie said then, deciding to be brutally honest. "I don't know what's going on with us right now, but I want to go back to how things were. A lot has changed, with me, obviously, but I know we can get through this." She reached for his hand, but he pulled it back.

"Look, Debs," and that use of her nickname cut through her, she couldn't deny that, "We're over. I'm sorry. It's not, you know," he gestured downward, at the missing part of her leg. "It's not you at all. It's my parents. They have a lot of plans for me, and I can't disappoint them. It ain't fair, but that's life, I guess."

Debbie frowned. "What sort of plans?" Whatever it was, surely, she could be a part of it—she could help in some way.

Jonas shrugged. "They need me on the farm. I don't have time for..." He didn't finish his sentence, but Debbie understood the gist of it. He didn't have time to play nursemaid. She was a hindrance now, a burden, no help to anyone.

"So... that's it?" Debbie asked, afraid of the answer, not wanting to hear it.

But the answer came anyway. "*Jah*. Sorry."

Just that. Two words and Debbie's world disintegrated even further. All the hopes she'd had, everything she'd been clinging to, fell apart.

Jonas got up, straightening his pants legs, and walked stiffly away. Debbie watched him go, her mouth slightly agape, tears burning in her eyes.

Moments later, Dawn was by her side. "Debbie? Are you okay? What did he say? Oh, I'm going to slap him!"

Debbie let her sister embrace her, leaned into her, and burrowed her face into her shoulder. "It's over," she said, her voice cracking on the last word, a sob releasing itself from her tight throat.

"He's horrid," Dawn said. "You know I don't like to insult people so freely, but that's what he is. You're better off without him."

Was she? Debbie didn't feel like she was. But even though Jonas was gone, she still had Dawn. That, at least, was something.

She sat up straight, wiped away her tears, and reached for her crutches. Dawn helped her back onto the cart, and they began the ride back home.

Chapter Six

Dawn was weeding the flowerbeds when she heard a cart pull up in the driveway behind her. She stood, turning to see who it was. Instantly, her face lifted into a smile. It was Jacob Peachey, climbing down from the seat of his family's buggy.

He smiled and waved as he approached, and Dawn's heart fluttered a little. She had always rather liked Jacob, not that she would ever have let him—or anyone else for that matter —know.

"*Gut* morning," he greeted her. "Hard at work, I see."

"A little," she said. "But I'm sure we can manage to make time for you."

He smiled at that, and Dawn's heartbeat quickened. "I thought I'd come and see how Debbie's doing," he said, and

Dawn felt her smile falter. Of course, he was there for Debbie; why would she have thought, or hoped for, anything else?

She nodded. "She's doing better," she said. "Let me see where she is."

Debbie sat at the kitchen table, a pestle in one hand with the other supporting the mortar. She was grinding dried mint leaves to replenish the tea stores. Several jars sat on the table in front of her. Chamomile leaves, peppermint, ginger, dried apple, and licorice root. She wished she could be outside with Dawn, cleaning out the hen house and weeding the driveway, with the sun on her back and the late summer breeze in her face. She'd always loved outdoors work best, loved to work beneath the wide, arching sky.

She wiped a stray tear from her face and tried to focus on her work. There was no point in wishing, and she was tiptoeing dangerously close to jealousy. Jealous of her own sister. What a life.

The peppermint ground, she tipped it into a small jar, and grabbed another handful of peppermint leaves from the bigger jar.

"Someone's working hard," Dawn said from behind her.

Debbie craned her neck to see her sister, dirt streaking her apron, her *kapp* a bit askew.

"Do you want to take a break? Jacob's here."

"*Nee*. I don't want to see anyone right now. But please thank him for coming." Debbie shook her head, although her heart lifted a little at the mention of Jacob. He'd been so good to them all the past few weeks, running errands for them, helping out with the yard work. He didn't have to do any of it, but he was here anyway. Far more than Jonas had done for them. *He* hadn't been to visit once, not even to ask if they needed anything.

Debbie had thought she'd be devastated at Jonas's cold rejection. For a few days, she hadn't wanted to get out of bed, had been unable to fully understand what had passed between them. And then she'd gotten angry. How *dare* he? First, he'd left her in the barn that day, run away while she was buried under rubble, and then, he'd *lied* about being there, and now *this*.

It was almost as though there were two of Jonas. The happy-go-lucky, funny and caring boy she'd known before the accident, and the callous, cold and cowardly one she'd been dealing with since. She loved the former but was enraged at the latter. How could someone be so different from himself? How could a person change so suddenly? Or, perhaps, she'd never really known him after all. She'd only seen the image he wanted to project, and now, finally, she was seeing the real Jonas, the self beneath the self.

She rubbed her forehead. All this thinking of Jonas was giving her a headache.

Dawn came back into the room. "I told Jacob that you preferred no company today. I think he's left." She frowned. "Are you okay?" She sat down beside Debbie.

Debbie set her work aside. "I'm okay," she said. "But I think I do need a break. Just a bit of fresh air."

"Do you want me to come with you?"

Debbie shook her head. "I'll manage," she said. She'd been getting on better with her crutches now, slightly more used to the imbalance she'd been experiencing. Although what she wasn't used to was the strange itching sensation that occasionally occurred below her stump. On those occasions, she felt as though her body was making fun of her, adding insult to literal injury.

She stood, supporting herself against the table, reached for her crutches, and then headed outside.

The driveway had been redone since she'd first gotten home. It was smoother now, easier to navigate with her crutches, and all the cracks in the paving had been filled in, too. She set a course for the old oak tree that stood, slightly stooped, at the bottom of the garden. Grass was harder to get across, the crutches sinking into the soft soil a little, but she managed okay and soon she was seated on the bench beneath the oak's large, outstretched arms.

She looked up into its boughs, at the golden light playing off the leaves, and wondered what God had in store for her now. *Please Gott,* she thought, *give me the strength to get through this, to cope with everything going on right now. Whatever it is you want from me, or for me, give me the strength to keep going.*

She sighed. She'd gotten through the last few weeks, barely. And most of that was down to Dawn, if Debbie was honest. Dawn's life had taken a backseat while she cared for her, and if Debbie was honest, she hated that. Not for herself, not out of pride, but because Dawn should be living her own life, not focused solely on hers. Debbie needed to find strength and a way to be independent, less for herself and more for Dawn's sake.

"Good afternoon," Jacob said, and Debbie looked up to see him smiling down at her. So, he hadn't left yet like Dawn had thought. It was funny, she thought, how little he looked like Jonas. Jonas was dark-haired, slight, and tall, where Jacob was fair and broad-shouldered, more like his uncle than his father. And yet, there was something in that smile that reminded her so strongly of Jonas, something that made her heart ache.

"Ah, Jacob. Dawn said you had come by."

"*Jah.* I just came to drop off some feed for the horses. Thought I'd stop for a minute and see how things are faring. I haven't seen you for a few days."

"*Jah*, well, I haven't felt up for visitors."

"Ah. Would you like me to leave you alone now?"

Debbie smiled. How like Jacob to ask that. He was too considerate for his own good, really. "*Nee*," she said. "I don't mind. Besides, it feels less and less like you're a visitor, you're here so often."

"I'd hope to think I'm at least a friend by now."

"Of course, you are. You've done so much for us. You'll always be a friend to this family. Certainly if *Mamm* has anything to do with it. She's always saying what a 'nice young man' you are."

Jacob's cheeks tinged with pink, and Debbie had to hold in a laugh.

It was nice, she thought, speaking naturally with someone outside of her family again. Jacob was easy to be around. She felt relaxed, almost content, sitting outside with the fresh breeze on her face and Jacob chatting beside her.

"Pardon?" she asked, having missed his last sentence.

"Will you come to church this Sunday?" he asked. She'd missed the last couple services, something she regretted. She should have made the effort, but she hadn't been able to face everyone's staring—hadn't wanted to leave the safety of her family home.

She nodded. Yes, she would attend preaching service this

Sunday. It was about time she started to get on with living her life again. And besides, she needed God with her now more than ever.

"I'll see you there, then," he said, getting up, and Debbie smiled. She would look forward to that.

Jacob left the Shelters' house feeling buoyed, light as air. He didn't even get irritated when Bandit tried to take the buggy left instead of right, or when he stopped entirely to munch a patch of long grass at the side of the road. Instead, an amused smile played at his lips. This horse had been driving him places since Jacob was ten years old. He deserved a bit of a break for those years of service.

Jacob thought about Debbie, how much better she'd seemed today, almost like her old self, composed, smiling, talkative. Jacob had barely been able to get a single sentence out of her the last few weeks. He hoped today was the new norm, that Debbie had passed the turning point and would continue to improve. She'd seemed pleased that they would meet again on Sunday, although Jacob couldn't read too much into that. Likely, she didn't feel for him that way. After all, his brother had been so cruel to her, why would she trust Jacob, or anyone, after that?

Still, he was thinking of asking her out for a drive, perhaps down to the river, or the park in town with its blossoming trees and fountains and ponds. He could imagine them sitting there, near the water, Debbie laughing. He loved the way she laughed, like it was from deep within. There was nothing superficial about her. She was honest and true, a good soul.

Stop thinking about her, he told himself, suddenly cross now. *It does you no good at all.* He tugged at the reins to get Bandit moving again, but the old horse just snorted and shook his head, then returned to his patch of grass.

Jacob sighed. He was going to have to wait.

Chapter Seven

Debbie couldn't help but be nervous. She'd missed two preaching services now, hadn't really been outside her family's property in all that time. This was the first time she would be out in public, would see other people. What would they think? What would they say?

Dawn was a solid presence beside her, their shoulders occasionally bumping as the buggy jolted. Debbie took strength from that. Whatever happened, her sister was beside her.

Dat parked the buggy with the others outside the Feldmann place. A few people were gathered outside. They'd gotten here early but clearly weren't the first ones to arrive. As Debbie lowered herself down from the buggy, unaided, and took her crutches from Dawn, she could feel eyes on her. She looked up and caught the whole group outside the Feldmanns' door staring at her. Some of them quickly glanced away, others didn't. They made their way over, and one of the women, Ellen, stepped forward, a sorrowful look on her face.

"Oh, Debbie, you poor thing," she said, and Debbie winced. "It's just dreadful what happened to you. We've all been keeping you in our prayers, of course."

Debbie forced a smile, but all she really wanted to do was turn and leave, get back into the buggy and ride home, and hole up in her room for the rest of the day. Instead, she said, "Thank you."

"We're very glad to see you," Isaiah Feldmann said, and that was better, at least, although Debbie noticed his eyes lowering to her covered stump under her skirts.

"Let's head inside," *Dat* said, much to Debbie's relief. "Get you settled in before the rabble arrive."

"Good idea," *Mamm* agreed, and Debbie followed them into the house.

Debbie sat with Dawn at the front of the unmarried women's section, and she leaned her crutches against the side of the bench.

"They mean well," Dawn said beside her.

Debbie nodded. She knew they did, but that didn't stop their comments and their stares from hurting.

"We'll go straight home after, I expect," she said, and Debbie hoped they would. She didn't want to stand around talking to people, receiving more pitying looks and exclamations of 'You poor thing!' She didn't want that, didn't want to be thought of as weak or damaged, like they no longer saw Debbie Shelter, and instead only saw what had happened to her, only saw her injury.

She took a deep breath, and as people began to filter into the large meeting room, she prayed silently to God, asking Him to give her strength. *I just need to get through today*, she thought. *Just today, just the next few hours.*

"Debbie." The bishop's voice was rich and warm. "Well, I'm very pleased to see you're back with us."

Debbie looked up at him. He was smiling. There was nothing pitying in his gaze, at least.

"We've all been praying for you," he said. "And judging by the color in your cheeks I'd say those prayers are slowly being answered."

Debbie didn't quite smile, but she nodded in quiet agreement.

"The last few weeks have been hard," she admitted, "but I'm taking things one day at a time."

"*Gut*," he said. "That's a very healthy attitude, I think. One foot in front of the... Goodness, that was the wrong phrase really, wasn't it?" He frowned. Debbie had never known the

49

bishop to fumble words before, and Debbie wanted to sink back, to become invisible.

"It doesn't matter," she said, wanting him now to go away, to leave her alone. If only they could *all* leave her alone.

And then Dawn's hand was on hers, her fingers curling around and squeezing tight. Debbie took strength from that. It was okay. She wasn't alone. Dawn was there.

"Well, anyway, we're all very glad you're back. I've picked out your favorite hymn to start."

He turned and headed to the front of the room.

Dawn leaned in, murmuring in her ear. "Did you see his face? He looked *horrified*. 'One foot in front of the other'. Honestly!"

Debbie giggled then. She had never seen him lose composure like that before. It *had* been sort of funny, she supposed.

She was glad when the service started, and she was able to lose herself in God's words, and in song. She loved to sing, she remembered, and the act made her feel both light and powerful. She had strength, she realized. She could, and would, endure. God, she was sure, loved her, and that was all she needed.

After the service had ended, they filed out, groups of people milling around to chat. Debbie wanted to get home, didn't want to wait around, but her parents were having some kind of deep discussion with the bishop, so she and Dawn stood slightly apart from everyone else, waiting.

Debbie could still feel eyes lingering on her, but no one was approaching

She could see Jacob nearer the house, standing with his parents, and then, emerging from the doorway, Jonas.

Debbie found that, despite her misery over him the past few weeks, seeing him now did nothing to her. He wasn't the person she'd thought he was. She saw him, now, for who he truly was. He smiled at her, and Debbie froze, a frown on her face. His smile faded, and he turned away.

That's right, Debbie thought bitterly. *Turn your back on anything you don't like, anything that makes you feel even a little bit uncomfortable.*

She turned to Dawn, who was watching her carefully. "Are you all right?" Dawn asked.

"Completely fine," Debbie said, sounding lighter than she felt.

"*Gut*. He's not worth any more tears," Dawn said, and Debbie was sure she was right.

They were spared any more discussion of Jonas Peachy by the arrival of Jacob. "How did you find the service?" he asked.

"It was lovely," Debbie said. "I feel so much better for having gone. I don't know why I missed the last couple." Except she did, really. Church itself *had* been good, but less so were the comments and the not-so-subtle looks. Still, church was worth that. And even now, even standing there waiting, seeing Jonas, she felt better than she had felt in a long while.

"I'm glad," Jacob said. "We've missed you here. Well, I know *I* have, so I'm sure everyone else has, too."

Debbie smiled. "That's kind of you to say," she said.

Jacob turned as his *mamm* called his name. "I think they need help setting up the tables for the meal, but I'll probably see you later?" The way he said it made it sound more like a question, and there was a hopeful note to his voice.

"You probably will," Debbie assured him.

He turned then, heading back toward his family, with one last glance over his shoulder. Debbie smiled at him.

Jacob was too good to them, she thought. He'd done so much for them. He was, without doubt, a much better person than his brother. Where Jonas had avoided any hardship, refused to go out of his way to even speak to her, Jacob had become invaluable to her and her family.

She couldn't help but feel a little glad that she would see him again soon.

Jacob was driving the buggy, trying not to listen to his parents' scolding.

"Honestly," his *mamm* was saying, "I don't know why you have to spend so much time with the Shelters. I'm sure after almost a month, they should be doing fine on their own."

"What your *mamm* means is, we need you on the farm," *Dat* interjected.

"Exactly."

Jacob gritted his teeth. "I'm *always* at the farm. And I do, what? A couple of hours work every other day for the Shelters. The rest of the time, I'm working on our farm, and, I'll add, working hard."

"All I'm saying is that your focus is divided," *Mamm* said, a slight whining tone in her voice now.

"What happened to *love thy neighbor?*" Jacob asked. "The Shelters have been through a lot lately, especially Debbie—"

"That girl. Honestly Jacob, I hope you're not getting any ideas about her. There are plenty of local girls we can—"

Jacob frowned. "Debbie *is* local. They've lived here for almost three years now."

"You know what I mean."

"*Jah*," Jacob said. "I know exactly what you mean. I'm sorry, but I think you can manage without me for a couple of hours a day. Besides, Jonas could always work more, eh, Jonas?"

Jonas just grunted, and Jacob suppressed a dirty look. The relationship between them had always been rocky, but these days they barely even spoke to each other. Jacob had made it clear exactly what he thought of Jonas, and instead of Jonas shaping up and making amends, he'd gone into an epic sulk that had lasted about two weeks now.

"Jonas has other things on his mind." *Mamm* sniffed.

Like courting Sarah Porter, Jacob thought. Funny, that his parents seemed to deem that more worthwhile than helping out neighbors in need.

"Suit yourself," Jacob said.

Once he'd parked the buggy and let Bandit loose in the field, he avoided his family, instead heading out to the woodshed. What he needed right now was some cathartic wood chopping. He took a log, stood it on the block, and raised the axe.

Down it came, slicing through the log and splitting it in two. He repeated the act, and slowly a pile of firewood began to form beside him.

Sweating, he wiped his brow and leaned the axe beside the block. He tucked the firewood inside the woodshed and sat down on the grass outside.

He knew his parents didn't appreciate the Shelters, including Debbie, because they'd come from Wisconsin. His mother was especially not keen on folks who hadn't been in Baker's Corner forever, but that wasn't going to stop him. He loved Debbie Shelter. He was sure of it. And now, he was more determined than ever to ask her out.

Chapter Eight

One crutch under her left arm, the other leaning against the wall of the chicken coop, Debbie grabbed feed from the pot she'd placed on the abutment and spread them out over the grass.

"Here you go," she said, scattering a pile of seed for the smallest of the hens. She stood in front of her while she ate, making sure the others didn't chase her away from the food. Her feathers were growing back after having been pecked out, and she made happy chirping noises as she ate.

Overhead, the sky was a pastel pink, the rising sun flecking the morning with gold. Debbie hadn't been up this early in a while. It was nice to see the sunrise again, the night fading and the light growing. And she'd missed this, the simple morning task of feeding the chickens.

Once the chickens had been fed, she carried the empty pot back by looping the handle over her wrist. In the shed, she placed it back into the feed bag. She began to tidy things—it was a mess of clutter in there, and she could barely see the workbench beneath the scattered tools and pieces of odds and ends.

An hour later, the shed looked much tidier. Perhaps now *Dat* could find the tools he needed straight away, instead of wasting so much time hunting through the jumble.

Feeling pleased with a job well done—or as well as she could manage it, at least—she headed back inside to put on a pot of tea. *Mamm* was already up, making breakfast, and she blinked hard at the sight of Debbie, no doubt surprised to see her up and about so early.

"Morning," Debbie greeted her, already busying herself with boiling a pot of water.

"*Gut* morning." *Mamm's* tone was cautious, like maybe this was too good to be true. "You're up early."

"Well, *jah*. Thought I'd grab the day for once."

"I hope you haven't been overdoing it," *Mamm* said, and Debbie felt an itch of irritation. Couldn't she just be glad that Debbie had managed to do something other than sit around all day?

"Don't worry," she said instead. "I only fed the chickens and tidied the shed up a little. Nothing too strenuous, I promise."

Mamm nodded then and turned back to the breakfast.

"Morning," Dawn said, yawning. She was fully dressed but not entirely awake yet, as she entered the room and took a seat at the table. "*Gut* to see I can take waking you up off my list of tasks for today," she mumbled.

"Glad to have helped," Debbie said, taking a seat. Standing for too long made her good leg ache a little, she found. Even after three weeks, almost a month, she didn't have enough strength in it to compensate. Dawn stood, taking over the tea-making without a word passing between them.

Once it was brewed, Dawn poured it out into four cups, and Debbie sipped hers slowly, holding the cup in both hands and savoring the warm feel. The day had dawned colder than usual, a sign summer was beginning to wane.

After breakfast, Debbie took the darning out onto the porch, to sit and work while everyone else got to work in the yard. The tasks of the day were weeding, wood-chopping, cleaning the chicken coop, and tending the pear orchard. Debbie wished she could be part of that. She loved the start of the harvest season, plucking that first crop of ripe fruit. Still, she would be able to help with the sorting and packing, she supposed.

There was always next year, she thought.

She was just finishing the darning when Jacob's buggy pulled up. "I heard you might need a hand, picking pears," he said, taking a seat beside her. "Although I must admit I'm planning on eating a few of them, too."

Debbie laughed a little and set aside the apron she'd finished fixing. "I think *Dat's* just finishing up the weeding. They'll all be back for the noon meal soon, and then they'll make a start."

Jacob raised an eyebrow. "Rather late in the day to start harvesting, isn't it?"

"I don't think there's too much to pick today, and I'm afraid we've become very relaxed about timing lately."

"Hmm. If they're not ripe yet, maybe I won't eat too many today then."

"Oh, I'm sure you'll be treated to a slice or two of *Mamm's* pear and blackberry pie soon enough," Debbie said.

Jacob rubbed his hands together eagerly. "I can't wait."

He really was very sweet, Debbie thought, watching the way his eyes crinkled at the corners. He was about six years older than she was, nearing twenty-five, she though. Mature, but not in a boring way. He had a sense of humor, and a sort of eagerness about him that Debbie couldn't help but like. She'd found herself looking forward to seeing him and wondered if perhaps that was the reason for her waking so early that morning.

Dawn cast them a glance as she walked up the steps to the

porch, and Debbie thought maybe there was something in that look, a flash of irritation or disapproval, and then it was gone. *What was that about?* Debbie wondered, but she didn't have the answer and didn't ponder it too seriously.

"Jacob," Dawn said, coming over. "Ready to pick a few pears with us?"

"Of course," he said. "I'm always ready."

Dawn smiled, and there was fondness there. Debbie was glad of that. Jacob had become important to their family, almost a part of it, in a way.

"I'll make us all some tea," Dawn said, "and then we'll be heading down to the orchard."

She went inside, leaving the two of them alone.

"Actually," Jacob said, drawing out the word. Debbie turned to face him again. "I was wondering..." he drew a breath, his blue-eyed gaze flicking away from her for just a second, and then back. "Maybe you'd like to take a drive with me sometime. We could go down to the river or something, have some lunch?"

Debbie faltered. She hadn't been expecting this. She knew Jacob cared about her, of course, but she hadn't known it was like that. After a long moment, she said, "I'm sorry, I can't."

It wasn't the answer she wanted to give, but it was the answer that came anyway. And it was the truth. How could she take a drive with Jacob when the last time she'd been out with a boy she'd nearly been crushed to death and ended up losing a limb? And after Jonas... No. She couldn't. It was better this way, she thought.

Jacob's face fell. He bit his lip, and then nodded. "I understand," he said.

Did he? Debbie wasn't sure he could possibly understand all of it, but she knew he was trying to be decent, not to let her feel bad. Not that it helped. She *did* feel bad.

He got up, then, and Debbie wanted to ask him not to leave, but she didn't, and he left. She watched him stride across the grass toward the pear orchard, and felt a small hollow opening up in her chest. *Come back,* she wanted to call, but she stayed quiet.

"Where did Jacob go?" Dawn asked, coming out of the house with two steaming cups of apple and ginger tea.

Debbie just shook her head and gestured vaguely in the direction he had gone.

Jacob stood in the orchard, surrounded by short pear trees, watching a crow tackle a half-rotten windfall. He'd finally gotten up the courage to ask Debbie out, and she'd said no. He shook his head at himself. *Of course,* she'd said no. It was only a month since her accident, as if she would feel up to going on a date. Besides, after what his brother had done, how could she trust him?

A nasty thought occurred to him then. Debbie had been in love with Jonas, he was fairly sure. What if she was *still* in love with him, after everything?

He sat down on a stump, dwelling on that for a while. *Nee*, he decided. How could she be in love with his brother, after everything? And she seemed to like Jacob, smiling when he came and sat with her. Of course, that didn't really mean much. As she'd said, he was a family friend now. She felt friendship for him, nothing more. He'd been a fool.

He raised his chin then. It didn't matter, he decided. He loved Debbie Shelter, and he would continue doing all he could for her, regardless of her feelings for him. Maybe, he thought, in time she would come to feel something more, and if not... Well, then he would have to deal with that, accept it and move on.

He got up off the stump as the Shelters approached, Joseph and Susanna side-by-side, followed by Dawn. He drew in a deep breath. They couldn't see how affected he was. He would walk tall, pick as many pears as he could for them, and he could dwell on things tonight when he was home in bed. But right now, there was work to be done.

Chapter Nine

Debbie half-turned in her bed, groaning and squinting open her eyes. There was a sharp pain in her leg. She sat up, leaning forward to massage it the way she would normally do when she had a cramp, and then stopped. The pain was in her left leg, below her stump. She frowned, annoyed with herself, with her body, for playing such a cruel joke, and lay back down again. She couldn't sleep—knowing it was a phantom pain made no difference, it still hurt—but she stayed in bed anyway, waiting for it to pass.

When it finally passed, she got out of bed, using her crutches to move to her wash basin, splashing herself with water before getting dressed.

She had an early appointment that morning, and Dawn was

already up and dressed by the time Debbie had made it out of her room. Dawn was humming to herself, making up a breakfast of fruit and toasted bread. Debbie realized then that it had been a while since she'd heard her sister sing, or anything close to it. Guilt wormed its way into her heart. Dawn had given up so much for her. She rarely went out with friends anymore or did activities she enjoyed. When was the last time she had gone to a singing?

"Thanks," Debbie muttered as Dawn passed her a plate. They sat down together—their parents had already eaten and gone out to start working in the orchard—and Dawn said a silent grace before they tucked into their food.

After breakfast, Dawn took Debbie to her appointment with the physiotherapist. Debbie always came away from those meetings feeling exhausted, and this was no different. Still she was happy to see Jacob's buggy outside the house when they got back, and she sat up a little straighter, feeling more awake than she had just moments before.

Jacob waved to them as they came up the drive. He was sitting on the porch with *Mamm* and *Dat*, drinking iced tea. Debbie took a seat across from him, beside her mother, while Dawn took the seat next to her.

"How's the picking?" Debbie asked, hoping her parents wouldn't ask her about the appointment in front of Jacob.

Dat nodded. "The season's starting nicely," he said. "This time next week we'll be working full days out there."

Debbie couldn't help but wonder how that might work without her. Jacob couldn't work for them full-time. He had his own family's farm to help take care of, and it was coming into the busy season for them all. He shouldn't be spending so much time there, but she couldn't deny she was glad he was. If her family couldn't manage the harvest without her help, that would only make her feel worse. At least with Jacob around, there was some kind of backup. A few hours or a day here and there was better than nothing.

And, she supposed, it wasn't as though she was sitting idle. She was darning, sewing, preserving, and preparing meals. All that was less for the rest of them to do, leaving them more able to focus on those other tasks.

"You'll stay for the noon meal, Jacob?" Dawn asked, and Debbie couldn't help but hope for him to say yes.

But he shook his head. "I've got to get back, I'm afraid. But certainly, another time."

Debbie felt the disappointment deep in her gut. Jacob was there every day, of course, but she felt like today she *needed* him to be here. She could use his good humor, that way he had of easing everything into perspective.

He didn't move right away though. He finished his lemonade, and while *Mamm* cleared some of the glasses, *Dat* took off toward the shed. Dawn lingered a moment, and then headed into the kitchen with the last of the glassware.

Debbie took a deep breath. "Perhaps," she said, trying to keep her nerve. "We could go for that drive sometime soon."

Gott, please let him say yes. Please don't let him have changed his mind.

Jacob blinked, his mouth half-opened. Then he said, "Sure. Whenever you like. There's no rush."

Debbie smiled, warmth spreading through her. He still wanted to. Even after she'd rejected him last time, he still wanted to take a drive with her, alone. She pushed her nervousness to the back of her mind. She wasn't going to let fear beat her. Not now, not ever.

"How about this Saturday?"

Jacob smiled. "Sounds *gut*." He pushed back his chair and stood. "I'll see you before then, I'm sure, but if not... definitely Saturday." He turned to call out a good-bye to *Mamm* and Dawn, and then headed down to his pony cart with a spring in his step. Debbie watched him strapping his horse into the harness, feeling hopeful, for the first time in a long while.

Jacob hadn't been able to wipe the grin off his face all day. He'd gone home from the Shelters' that afternoon feeling as light as air. He'd hummed to himself as he weeded the front yard and wheeled sheep excrement from the top paddock to the compost heap.

He paused, the last wheelbarrow of the day full to the brim, the sun setting, turning the sky a fiery red. He watched it go down for a while, feeling like good things were coming his way. He turned and took the wheelbarrow up the slope to the compost heap, dumped it, and headed inside to wash up before supper.

Everyone else was already there. They must have finished the fencing in the lower fields a little while ago, because dinner smelled as though it was almost ready.

"You look happy," his mother commented as he tried to creep past. There was a question in her voice—she clearly wanted to know the reason why.

"Shouldn't I be?" Jacob asked, unable to wipe the smile off his face.

"Well, it's very nice that you are, it just seems a bit unusual of late."

Interesting, he thought. He'd never thought of himself as an unhappy person, but when was the last time he'd felt this good? Not in a long while, he thought. Probably long before his brother had started dating the woman he was keen on, that was certain.

"Well then," he said, grinning wider. "You'd better make the most of it."

He passed Jonas on the stairs and stopped humming to himself instantly. Jonas only glared at him. Jacob opened his mouth to say something but closed it again. Harsh words weren't needed today, and besides, not even Jonas could ruin his good mood today. "Good evening, brother," he said.

Jonas only grunted and continued past him.

Well then. That was his prerogative, Jacob supposed.

He washed up, scrubbing under his nails before he headed back down for dinner. His place was already laid up when he got to the table, *Mamm* just setting down the last dish, a baked ham.

His father led them in silent prayer, and then Mamm started the dishes of food around the table.

"How are the Shelters?" Jonas asked.

Jacob stared at him for a moment. Jonas's tone had been innocent enough, even pleasant, but he *knew* it was a bone of contention between Jacob and their parents. Jacob shook himself out of his disbelief, forcing himself to be pleasant. He couldn't always assume the worst of his brother, he supposed.

"They're well," he said. "Debbie seems much better, much more like herself."

"Did you get a lot of work done?" Jonas asked, and there was a sly note to his voice now that Jacob didn't like.

"Quite a bit, yes. How was the fencing?"

Dat nodded. "We've gotten most of it done. Might have managed the whole thing, if you'd been around to help." He coughed, then, seeming to remember himself. "But never mind now. Things out there look much better."

"I should hope so. That took me almost four hours," Jonas said.

"Pernicious thing, that ragwort," *Dat* said. "I hope you got all the root out, too."

"I think so," Jonas said, then corrected himself. "Well, I made sure of it."

"*Gut.* We don't want *that* coming back up again."

Conversation ebbed a little after that, and they ate in silence for a while, the men occasionally commenting on how good Mary's cooking was.

After a while, Jonas asked, "So what *were* you in such a good mood about earlier? Singing to yourself and everything. Quite unlike you, brother. You're usually so grumpy."

Maybe around you, Jacob thought.

Dat said, "Jonas, don't pry," and that was the end of *that* conversation.

Jacob quickly shoved a piece of ham into his mouth, so he

didn't chuckle out loud. Still, he couldn't help smiling to himself. His brother had, for once, been put in his place, and *he* was finally going to go out with Debbie Shelter. Things were certainly looking up.

Chapter Ten

It was a few days later that Jacob called by to take Debbie for a ride. It wasn't exactly a secret affair—it couldn't be, really, given Debbie's circumstances. Debbie had made sure she knew where they were going, and that her whole family knew about it, just in case something happened. She felt that she could trust Jacob and knew, really, that nothing was going to happen. She understood that the incident in the barn had been a one in a million chance but knowing was not the same as feeling.

Watching the buggy pull up was an unsettling feeling. The Peacheys only had one, so of course, it was the same buggy that had taken her and Jonas to the barn that day. Not that she hadn't seen it a hundred times since then, but she hadn't been going to ride in it before now.

That unease faded as soon as Jacob smiled at her. Then her heart fluttered, and she felt excited all over again. The nervousness was still there, but it was mixed now, overlaid with this other, new emotion. She stood slowly, using one crutch, and waited for Jacob to near the porch.

Dawn had been in a bad mood all morning, but she came outside now, probably having heard the buggy approach.

"*Dat* says you're to be home by five," she said. "He'll be starting up a search party if you're not."

Debbie knew she wasn't joking either. Rather than setting her on edge, that warning relaxed her, took the edge off her fear. Her family was looking out for her. They all knew where she was going, what route they were taking, and of course, who she was with.

"Thanks," she said, smiling at Dawn with appreciation.

Dawn smiled back, but it seemed a little forced. Debbie hoped she wasn't worried, as that had to be it. Dawn had become almost a third parental figure since the barn accident. It wasn't what either of them had wanted, but there it was.

"I'll be fine," Debbie assured her.

"I know," Dawn said, and flashed that smile again, meant to be reassuring but not quite matching the unhappy look in her eyes. She turned to Jacob. "Take good care of her."

"I promise I will," Jacob said, and that was all either of them needed. Jacob's word was good. After all he'd done for them, Debbie felt they could trust that.

Although Jacob had gotten out of the buggy and offered his arm, Debbie made her own way to the buggy with her crutches, taking it slow and making sure they were solid on the loose gravel before she put her weight down on them. She accepted his help up onto the buggy, though, and thanked him.

He settled next to her and took the reins in his hands. "You're okay?" he asked. "If you change your mind, we'll come right back."

Debbie nodded, grateful for those words. "Thank you," she said, "But I'm okay."

He smiled at her then, a look of fondness in his eyes that caught her off guard for a minute. As they drove through the countryside, she gazed around them at the wheat and corn fields, the crows making black marks against the blue sky. She loved this little corner of the world. She'd only lived here a few years, but already, it was home.

She snuck glances at Jacob occasionally, wondering how she felt about him. She'd grown rather fond of him these last few weeks, come to look forward to his visits, to appreciate his jokes and to love his smile—the way his blue eyes crinkled at the corners. She wanted to brush a hand over the freckles that dusted his nose and cheeks. *That* feeling was new, at least, catching her by surprise. She quickly looked away from him, not wanting him to catch her staring.

Jacob pulled the buggy over by the river. He helped her down and then grabbed a picnic basket from the back. Debbie stared at it for a moment. She wasn't sure why she hadn't expected a picnic. It was lunchtime, after all. But there was an actual basket, that hinted of something more than just hastily put together sandwiches wrapped in cloth. It suggested that Jacob had put a great deal of actual thought into today.

Jacob picked out a spot close to the bank, with a small wooden loveseat facing the water. Debbie was glad that it was a different spot to where Jonas had broken up with her. That bench had faced away from the river, this one was far prettier. She took a seat and gazed out over the water that was gently rippling in the breeze.

"This is my favorite spot," Jacob said, his tone thoughtful. "Whenever I have to think about something important, this is where I come."

"It's lovely," Debbie agreed.

"Are you hungry?" Jacob asked, gesturing to the picnic basket.

Debbie didn't have to think about her answer; she nodded immediately. It was past midday, and her stomach had been rumbling quietly on the drive over.

Jacob opened the basket, a wicker and cloth construction with metal hinges, and handed Debbie a plate. He then began opening jars and unwrapping things, laying them on her plate for her. There were cold cuts, cheese, spreads, and small savory pies. She could also see fruits and slices of cake.

"This looks wonderful *gut*," she said, staring down at her plate. "You've put a lot of effort into this, I can see."

Jacob waved a hand. "Nonsense. I just threw a few things together, that's all. Most of it is leftovers. I mean... I suppose I shouldn't be so honest there. You thought I was wonderful there for a minute, didn't you?"

Debbie laughed. "You *are* wonderful, Jacob Peachey. Honestly, everything you've done for us... You're a *gut* man." She blushed, then, hoping she hadn't said too much.

"Shall we pray," he suggested and bowed. She joined him in the silent prayer, and when he cleared his throat, signaling the end of the prayer, she looked up.

Debbie murmured, "Amen," and began to eat.

Jacob dropped Debbie home at half past four. They could have stayed out a little later, but he didn't want Debbie's parents to worry about her, and he knew they would have if he'd played it too close to the hour.

He walked Debbie to the porch, catching her when she almost fell, holding her for just a second longer than he needed to, caught up in the smell of her, like lavender, and the warmth of her waist under his hand. Her cheeks went pink, and he moved away a little, staying just close enough that she could lean on him if she needed—or wanted—to.

Debbie smiled at him as they reached the porch, acting shy, back to her nervous self from earlier. She was cute, he thought. He'd always found her beautiful, but he'd never seen this hesitant, uncertain side of her before. She'd always seemed so sure of herself, almost to the point of bluntness at times. Even after the accident, she'd been withdrawn, unhappy, maybe anxious at times, but not *shy*.

"I've had a really nice afternoon," Debbie said. "I enjoy spending time with you, Jacob Peachey. You're quite good company."

Jacob laughed. "Am I? That's a new one. I always thought people found me a bit boring."

Debbie shook her head. "Not at all. You make me laugh."

"Well, then that's all the skill I need in life." Jacob half-meant that, too. There was no higher honor, he felt, that to be the one making Debbie Shelter laugh.

Jacob returned home that evening feeling as though everything was finally right with the world. The picnic had gone well, and Debbie had seemed to genuinely enjoy herself. For the most part, she'd been laughing, chatty, just like her old self again. Yes, she'd seemed unsure at first, but after a while, she'd relaxed. And she'd said she liked being with him.

"You're going out with Debbie Shelter?" Jonas's tone was scathing, as though he thought Jacob had somehow lowered himself. Jacob groaned internally. How had he found *that* out? Jacob hadn't thought anyone except the Shelters knew about it.

" Noah Eicher said he'd seen you by the river together. Very romantic, he thought. I thought *I* was supposed to be the younger brother getting your hand-me-downs."

Jacob stared at him for a moment, not wanting to believe Jonas had actually said that. But he hadn't misheard.

"Jonas," he said, deciding that enough was enough. They needed to resolve this, now, before it grew into something bigger. "I know I was harsh to you, but harsh words were needed, you do know that? You know that what you did was so wrong—beyond wrong. Running away, lying..."

"Lying?" Jonas said, putting on an affronted expression.

"*Jah*, brother. Lying through your teeth!"

Jonas scowled. "I have no idea what you're talking about," he said, turning on his heel. He walked away, back straight, head held high—proud. Jacob sighed. He didn't know how to get through to his brother—everything he did or said just seemed to make things worse.

Jacob stayed that evening in his room, torn between happiness over his date with Debbie, and anger and frustration over his exchange with Jonas. Was it *his* fault, something *he'd* done to make Jonas so bitter toward him? Surely, Jonas saw that what he'd done after the barn had collapsed was wrong. Maybe Jacob *had* judged too harshly, been too cold toward him. He sighed. He wasn't wrong, he decided, to find Jonas' attitude repulsive. Still, he missed how things had been before. They'd quarreled plenty, yes, but they'd laughed together too, shared jokes that no one else understood. He missed his brother, almost as much as he was angry with him.

Chapter Eleven

It was almost a full week before Debbie went out with Jacob again. He had been busy, he said, with his parents' farm, and of course with helping Debbie's family on *their* land, too. Debbie wondered if Jacob ever actually got time to eat and sleep, with everything he did. But when she asked, he assured her he managed just fine. "Besides," he said, his tone joking, "who needs food and sleep when I have you?"

"You think you have me?" Debbie said, raising her eyebrows.

"Well, for the next few hours I do," Jacob said with a shrug, although the confidence had ebbed slightly from his voice.

This time, they went to the park in town, the only Amish amongst the strolling, playing and jogging *Englischers*. They attracted a few stares, but not many, and besides, both Jacob and Debbie were only too used to it. They sat on a bench by the large fountain, watching the ducks swim. They ate cold cut sandwiches and strawberries and talked about the harvest season which was well underway. In fact, they talked about all the subjects either of them could think of—family, friends, local news, even books.

It was pleasant, Debbie thought, to talk about something other than how she was, how she was coping. That subject didn't even come up at all, and Debbie found that, just for a little while, she was able to feel like her old self, like more than just her injury.

When the first few drops of rain began to fall, they both looked up. A raindrop splashed between Jacob's eyes and ran down his nose. "Time to go," he said, regret heavy in his voice.

"We could stay a while," Debbie said, not wanting the day to end just yet. "Wait it out under the pagoda over there."

Jacob followed her gesture and, after a moment, agreed. They moved beneath the shelter as a light sheet of rain fell across the park, emptying it of its visitors. They were now, alone, just them and the sound of the rain pattering on the metal roof.

Jacob slipped his arm around her waist, and Debbie rested her head against his shoulder, looking out at the damp grass, the dripping tree limbs. Finally, Jacob sighed, and Debbie raised her head.

"I don't think Bandit will be very happy if we leave him out in this too long," he said, and Debbie had to agree. It wasn't really fair to the poor old thing if they stayed under this shelter while he was out in the rain getting soaked.

So, they called it a day, and Jacob drove Debbie home.

Still, even after he had left, Debbie could feel the warmth of his arm around her, the smell of his skin and his clothes, the way his fingers had shifted over her waist.

Was she beginning to fall for him? she wondered idly as she got ready for bed. Maybe. Maybe, she was.

Chapter Twelve

"Debbie, can I speak to you for a moment?" Jonas's voice caught Debbie off-guard. She'd seen him inside the house, of course, during the preaching service, but he'd come out ahead of them, and she hadn't seen him when she and Dawn had exited the barn. She'd assumed he'd left already and hadn't been particularly sorry for that.

She looked at him for a minute, wary, then nodded.

"Uhm, I mean... alone?" he said, glancing to Dawn, who stood with her arms folded over her chest and her eyebrows raised.

Debbie looked to Dawn, who looked back at her.

"Go ahead," Dawn said after a moment, her tone both annoyed and exasperated. She uncrossed her arms and stalked to a spot a several feet away, giving them a little privacy, but not too much.

"Look, Debs—"

Debbie cut him off. "Please don't call me that anymore. It's Debbie, or, if you like, Deborah."

He grinned, and that look caught her off guard. The old Jonas was back, the fun, mischievous one she had shared so many private jokes with. "Not Miss Shelter, then?"

Debbie set her jaw, refusing to be pulled in to whatever game Jonas was playing. "What did you want to say to me, Jonas?"

He sighed, seeming awkward all of a sudden. He scraped the toe of his shoe across the pavement, then stopped. "Look, Debbie, I'm sorry for everything that happened between us."

Debbie raised a brow. Was he seriously apologizing? After all this time? She studied his expression, trying to determine whether he was sincere or not. Strangely, he did look sincere. She let out her breath. "Thank you," she said curtly.

"So you can forgive me?"

She raised her chin slightly. "I've been working to forgive you, Jonas. I have. But I will tell you this, it hasn't been easy."

He chewed the inside of his lip.

She continued to look at him, almost glad for the chagrin on his face. Then she realized that she did want to forgive him. If not for his sake, then for hers.

"I do forgive you," she said, forcing the words. "I can't imagine why you did what you did. I truly can't. But I'm putting that all in the past now. Things are different. *I* am different."

He nodded. For a quick second, Debbie had the impression he was going to reach out and take her hand, but the moment passed.

"*Jah*, you're different," he said, then, "Look, Debs—sorry, Debbie. I was wrong to break up with you like that. You're amazing, Debbie. Everything you've been through... I can see now it's only made you stronger. Since you forgive me... Well, I was wondering... Um, I can call for you this weekend, if you like. We could go for a drive someplace, like old times?"

Debbie gaped at him, incredulous. This, she had not expected. Was Jonas Peachey really asking to court her again, after what he'd done? Forgiveness was one thing, but this...?

Not so long ago, it would had been everything she wanted, but now, it made her stomach turn over, and she had trouble even responding.

"Well?" he asked, giving her that charming smile she'd always imagined was just for her. That charming smile that could cut through any reservations she had.

It threw her. Confused her.

"I... I..." she stammered.

"Just think on it." Jonas's expression was hard to read, but he nodded, and then bid her a good day.

"What was that about?" Dawn asked suspiciously, coming close again.

"Uh, nothing. I don't think," Debbie said, struggling to make sense of what had just happened. She wouldn't keep their conversation a secret from Dawn for long, but hopefully enough time to think it over in peace, without Dawn's input. Yes, she would think about it, like Jonas suggested. Then she would discuss everything with Dawn.

That night, Debbie lay awake in bed. It was almost midnight, and she'd been unable to sleep, mulling things over in her mind until everything just became jumbled and confused. One minute she wanted to spit in Jonas's face. The next minute, she was deeply ashamed of such volatile feelings. And then the minute after that, she remembered how much she had loved Jonas—the fun they'd had together.

She wasn't sure what she felt anymore. She had loved him, yes, but as she'd told him earlier, so much had changed since then. She'd seen a different side of him. A side she didn't like at all.

A side she was ashamed of. She'd changed, too, she supposed. How could she not have, after everything?

And of course, there was Jacob, who had been so good to her. Jacob was sweet, sensitive and kind, everything his brother wasn't. Jonas, Debbie was sure, only ever really thought of himself. Deep in her heart, she'd always felt that, even when they'd been courting. They'd always done what *he* wanted to do, and he'd never really listened to her, not that day in the barn, and not before.

No, she decided, suddenly. She couldn't take Jonas back. How could she, after everything? Besides, she didn't want to. She didn't want *him*. And she could only too well imagine the look on Dawn's face if she went back to Jonas. She laughed, then, the sound cutting through the quiet night. She slapped a hand over her mouth, before remembering everyone else was asleep upstairs—they wouldn't have heard her.

No. Her time with Jonas had been good while it had lasted, but she knew too much about him now to think she could change him. Because he would have to change for her to ever love him again.

Although she could forgive him, she would never be able to fully trust him. He hadn't just lied, he had shunned and ignored her ever since the accident, an accident he had run away from, leaving her there, injured and alone. He probably hadn't even thought about her; he'd just run out of there to save his own neck without looking back. And what he done to make up for it? Nothing.

Whereas Jacob... Jacob had done so many things for her family since she'd gotten out of the hospital. He had run errands for them, helped with the pear harvest, cleaned out the chicken coop—and countless other little things. She felt safe with Jacob. She could trust his word, because he always kept it, even about the little things.

How could two brothers be so different from each other, she wondered? They'd had the same upbringing, the same genes, and yet they'd turned out to be almost opposites. There were similarities there, of course, but where it counted, in their hearts, they were not the same at all.

And Jacob...? She wasn't sure whether she loved him, exactly, not yet, but there was something between them, wasn't there? She wanted to explore that, to see where it led them.

Her mind made up, she closed her eyes and finally fell asleep.

The following morning Debbie washed and dressed and headed down the hallway to the kitchen. No one else was up yet. She put on the tea, but before she could start making breakfast, Dawn appeared in the doorway. She was bright-eyed and neat, and she smiled at Debbie.

Debbie smiled back. "Tea?"

"Please," Dawn said, already beginning to cut fruit for their breakfast.

"Jonas wants me back," Debbie said, deciding she might as well tell Dawn everything now.

"*Nee!*" Dawn said loudly, her hand pausing with the knife in the air. "Please Debbie, tell me you said *nee*."

"Truth be told, I was so stunned, I could hardly speak. He told me to think about it. Well, I have thought about it. I don't want him back. Don't worry. I couldn't possibly take him back."

Dawn blew out her breath with relief and resumed cutting the apple waiting on the chopping board. "*Gut*," she said. "I wouldn't have allowed it anyway."

Debbie chuckled. "Oh, wouldn't you have?"

"*Nee*," Dawn said, her tone firm. "You're far too *gut* for the likes of Jonas Peachey."

"But Jacob, on the other hand..."

Dawn was quiet for a moment, and she looked tense. "*Jah. Jah*, I'd say he's *gut* enough."

Debbie smiled, a tight feeling in her chest. Tears welled in her eyes, and she blinked them back.

"And you," she said. "You're the best thing in my life, Dawn. I'm so glad I have you as a sister."

Dawn made a scoffing noise, but she put down the knife, turned, and crossed the few feet toward her sister. She threw her arms around Debbie, pulling her close. Debbie could smell her soap, the faint scent of lavender on her clothes from the sachet she kept in her drawers. She hugged Dawn back.

"I love you, Debbie," Dawn said. "And I'm here, no matter what. You know that, don't you?"

If Debbie hadn't known it before the accident, she certainly did now. Dawn had done everything for her, been there when even her parents had found things overwhelming. Dawn had made everything seem achievable, had helped the horror to settle down into a new kind of normal. Debbie loved her sister for that. She always would.

"Well, this is nice," *Mamm* said from the doorway.

Debbie turned to see a smile on her face. When was the last time she had seen *Mamm* smile so freely?

"You girls, always so close." Her tone was fond as she crossed the room to the pantry, grabbing the potatoes to peel.

Soon they were all sat around the table, eating and talking as normal. It was nice, Debbie thought. Breakfast with her family. She'd missed a lot of breakfasts, hiding away in her room, not wanting to be part of anything. She wouldn't miss any more, she decided. This life was hers, and she was going to live it, no matter what.

Debbie met Jonas by the river, at the same place he had first broken up with her, the place where she had first realized that Jonas Peachey was not the man she'd thought him to be.

He looked good, she thought absently, well-rested, like he hadn't had many sleepless nights lately. Unlike Debbie, who had tossed and turned every night for the past month, unable to shut off her thoughts, unable to get comfortable enough to sleep deeply.

He greeted her warmly, his smile confident and almost jaunty. "Well?" he said. "Did you think about it?"

"I did," Debbie said. "And I've decided against it. I can forgive you for everything that's happened, Jonas, but there is simply no way in the world I can ever trust you again."

His smile disappeared, morphing into a scowl. She had seen that look on his face before, whenever she had disagreed with him.

"Suit yourself," he said with a shrug. "I was just trying to be nice."

Debbie leaned back, away from him, heat flushing her cheeks. She felt as though she'd just been slapped. Had he really just said that? She closed her mouth, aware it was hanging slightly open.

"Jonas Peachey," she said, anger now vibrating through her words, "you are the absolute opposite of *nice*. I feel sorry for you, and I feel sorry for whoever you court and marry."

She squared her shoulders, pulled her crutches toward her, rose slowly, and stalked off up the slope, her head held high, toward the buggy where Dawn waited for her.

As Dawn helped her up, her anger faded into a sense of calm. She was, finally, completely and absolutely done with Jonas Peachey.

Debbie had had an appointment that morning, to discuss again the possibility of having a prosthesis fitted. This time, she had come to a decision, at least for now. She didn't want the prosthesis. Perhaps, in a year or two, she would change her mind and have one fitted, but for now, she felt she had been managing okay with her crutches. A prosthetic leg was not a 'fix', she had felt, and besides that, it was horrifically expensive. She knew her family couldn't afford it, not just now, so if she didn't *need* it, then she would just make do without. And she certainly didn't want to drain the district's emergency fund. And the cost of a prosthesis would certainly do just that.

She sat in her usual seat on the porch that afternoon, mending the hem of Dawn's *kapp* and two of her father's shirt buttons, which had come off again. She had just finished sewing on the second button, when Jacob's buggy pulled up, his old horse tossing his head from side to side, clearly not in the mood to be working on such a fine, warm day.

Jacob leapt down from the driver's seat and almost immediately lost his balance, stumbling and putting out a hand to support himself. His cheeks turned pink, and Debbie stifled a laugh, less at the fall and more at his embarrassment. She knew how that felt, at least.

Her face relaxed into a fond smile as he approached and took a seat beside her. "How are you today?" he asked. He eyed the finished clothes in her lap. "Busy?"

"Not anymore," she said.

"Well, *gut*. Because I definitely feel I should be the center of all your attentions."

Debbie laughed. "Oh, do you now?"

"I do. And do you know why?"

Debbie shook her head. She was sure he was about to tell her.

"Because," he said, "you're the center of all of my attention."

His face split into a grin, and she felt her own expression lifting to match it. He leaned toward her, then, and lightning quick, planted a kiss on her cheek.

She raised a hand to her cheek, her fingers gently feeling the spot where his mouth had been. She smiled up at him. "Well, you certainly have caught my attention now."

Jacob laughed, and Debbie's heart felt full in that moment. Yes, Jacob Peachey certainly did have her attention now, and likely would for a long time to come.

The End

Continue Reading...

Thank you for reading **Dismissing Debbie! Are you wondering what to read next?** Why not read **The Secret Courtship?** Here's a peek:

"I'm telling you, Bridget, it was David."

"And he was picking up a girl in town? I don't believe it. It was probably one of his cousins, Esther. You know his father has twelve brothers, right? And his mother has four brothers and four sisters. Two great big Amish families. It had to be a relative he was picking up. I mean, who else could it be?"

"She didn't act like they were related. The girl slid over on the seat right next to him. It looked more like he was taking her out for a ride. If you ask me, they looked right cozy."

"Well, I didn't ask you, so I don't know why we're even talking about it." Bridget's voice was harsher than she intended.

"I-I thought you'd want to know, Bridget—since you and David have been secretly engaged for months. And didn't you just tell me the other day that as soon as you're baptized, the two of you are going to marry? *That's* why I'm telling you this. Do you really think he should be riding around with other girls?"

"It was one of his cousins. You're making a mountain out of a molehill, Esther. And I don't want to talk about it anymore. It's nice of you to look out for me. But, please, it's really ridiculous to think David was out riding with another girl."

"Aren't you even going to ask him about it?"

"What for? He did nothing wrong."

"Bridget! He was out riding with someone else. I *saw* him." Esther was clearly exasperated.

"When was it?"

"Friday. My *mamm* and I were leaving the Flea Market. It was around five o'clock. David pulled up to the Flea Market exit, and there was an Amish girl waiting there. I didn't know her, but she climbed up into the buggy, and they drove off. They passed right in front of us. I waved, but he didn't see us. The girl had red hair—I saw it plain as day under her *kapp*."

Bridget Lehman shook her head. She was losing patience with

her cousin Esther's suspicions about David. "*Nee*. I'm not going to worry about this, and I think you should just forget about it, too."

Esther said nothing, and the girls continued on their way home from their jobs at their mothers' co-owned fabric shop. Their mothers were sisters, and Esther and Bridget had been practically raised together. Since early childhood, they'd told each other everything. All of their secrets, dreams, and ambitions were known only to themselves, each other, and God.

But right then, Bridget sincerely wished she'd never said a word to Esther about her and David.

VISIT HERE To Read More:

http://www.ticahousepublishing.com/amish-miller.html

Thank you for Reading

If you **love Amish Romance, Click Here:**

https://amish.subscribemenow.com/

to find out about all **New Hannah Miller Amish Romance Releases! We will let you know as soon as they become available!**

If you enjoyed ***Dismissing Debbie!*** would you kindly take a couple minutes to leave a positive review on Amazon? It only takes a moment, and positive reviews truly make a difference. I would be so grateful! Thank you!

Turn the page to discover more Hannah Miller Amish Romances just for you!

More Amish Romance from Hannah Miller

Visit HERE for Hannah Miller's Amish Romance:

http://www.ticahousepublishing.com/amish-miller.html

About the Author

Hannah Miller has been writing Amish Romance for the past seven years. Long intrigued by the Amish way of life, Hannah has traveled the United States, visiting different Amish communities. She treasures her Amish friends and enjoys visiting with them. Hannah makes her home in Indiana, along with her husband, Robert. Together, they have three children and seven grandchildren. Hannah loves to ride bikes in the sunshine. And if it's warm enough for a picnic, you'll find her under the nearest tree!

Made in the USA
San Bernardino,
CA